LILLIE
OF WATTS

A Birthday Discovery

by *Mildred Pitts Walter*

illustrated by *Leonora E. Prince*

THE WARD RITCHIE PRESS · LOS ANGELES

jW17L1

*Dedicated to my sons, Lloyd and Craig
and my good friend, Deonne*

*With a special debt of gratitude to Dick and Mary Lewis and
Silvia Richards, whose encouragement made the book possible;
the members of the Watts Writers' Workshop; Louise Meriwether,
workshop instructor; and Budd Schulberg, workshop founder.*

LILLIE awoke with a good feeling. Today she was eleven years old. Finally, Mr. Knox would play "Happy Birthday" to her on his violin. She would put on her best skirt and sweater, comb her hair pretty and get to school early to help her teacher. She liked to help Mr. Knox. He was the first man teacher she had ever had. He was also the best.

Mr. Knox knew an awful lot, Lillie thought. But sometimes he could say some funny things—like the time when he had said all children have birthday parties! All the boys and girls laughed. Nobody had had a birthday party in that room. As Mama always said, who could afford it?

It was good to get out of bed before anybody else was up. While she was taking the curlers out of her hair she thought how nice it would be to have long, soft hair like that girl she had seen in the health film at school. The film was in color. It showed a girl Lillie's age washing her hair, cleaning her room, and choosing the right clothes. The girl had long red hair. No wonder she was chosen as an example of a healthy student.

Lillie kept thinking, why didn't Mama listen to her? There were so many things on television advertised to

Lillie wished her hair was long and pretty, instead of short and over-curled.

make hair long and pretty. That's all they talked about— does she or doesn't she? Do blondes have more fun? But all Mama ever said was, "Lillie, you pretty enough already. They don't mean us when they doing all that talking about hair. Forget that television. Besides, you just a baby."

A baby! She was eleven years old today, and Mr. Knox said she was tall for her age.

Lillie took all the curlers out and looked in the mirror. There was her same hair, now over-curled. She pushed it with her fingers, teasing it to frame her small, dark brown face with big, bright brown eyes. As she looked at her image she wondered why so many people said she was pretty and intelligent.

What is intelligent? She wondered, and how can one look intelligent? She would ask Mr. Knox. He would like that question. He would take a long time to answer, and she could help him clean the room while he explained.

Lillie liked the early morning best. Everybody was sleeping. The house was quiet, and she could think about herself, about school, and about Mrs. Byrd for whom Mama worked.

Tomorrow was Saturday, and there was no school. She would have a special treat. Mama had promised to take her to Mrs. Bryd's in Malibu. Right down on the ocean—that's where Mrs. Byrd lived. Lillie had never been there, but she knew what it would be like. The ocean was Mrs. Byrd's front yard. The whole ocean! All beautiful blue-green and white when the sun was shining, and foamy grey and white on a cloudy day.

Mama said that being at the ocean was like being in a

thunder-storm without having to be afraid. She liked the BOOM BOOM sounds the way Mama did them. One time she heard the sound in a seashell that Mama brought home. Her heart pounded. She was happy, for at last, to-morrow, she would see the ocean. On Monday, at sharing time in school, she would tell her classmates all about it. The sounds, the colors, the sand—everything.

She would remember everything about Mrs. Byrd's house. She would tell them that Mr. and Mrs. Byrd had three bedrooms for just the two of them. In Lillie's house there were three bedrooms, also, but for eight people. Would be nine if Daddy were still living. She and Mama and Eddie shared one room. Eddie was six and her only brother. Her two older sisters, Evelyn and Joyce, shared a room upstairs. And Rosemary, the oldest sister, had a room upstairs, too, with her husband, Tyrone, and their baby, Michael.

Lillie was glad Mama slept so soundly, and Eddie did, too. That made it easy for her to slip out of bed and think all by herself. She thought how glad she would be when Rosemary got her own apartment. Then she, Lillie, could have a room all to herself. Rosemary's husband left early in the morning to go to his regular job. When he finished there, he went on to a second job at a filling station. Lillie often heard Rosemary complain about the long hours Tyrone had to work. Then Mama would tell her to be patient. It was hard to get by on just one job. Rosemary should be thankful Tyrone had two jobs when so many men in Watts didn't have one.

Mama always said Rosemary should have thought

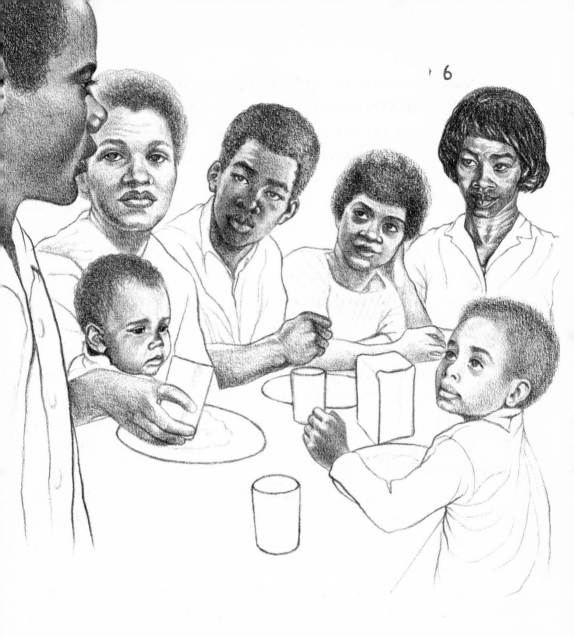

When she walked into the kitchen everyone stopped talking and looked at her in amazement.

about how bad things would be before she married Tyrone. She was only seventeen when she got married and Tyrone was only nineteen. He had finished Jordan High, and Mama was glad about that. But it sure was taking them a long time to get that apartment.

Too much thinking. Lillie decided she had better wake Mama to get breakfast and be off to work. She had to be on the job at nine. Malibu was a long way from Watts. Lillie woke Mama. After Mama had gone downstairs to start breakfast, Lillie finished dressing for school.

The smell of frying meat and the noise in the kitchen reminded her she'd better hurry. She was hungry. The last one at the table got the least to eat.

When she walked into the kitchen everyone stopped talking and looked at her in amazement. She had on her bright red-orange sweater and plaid skirt that matched. She looked good in bright colors. Her teachers all said so. Mrs. Byrd had sent that sweater, especially for her, and Mama had bought the skirt. It was her nice outfit for special occasions.

They were waiting for Mama to send her back upstairs to take off her only good clothes, to braid her hair, and come down for school today like all days.

Lillie looked at Mama and smiled.

"Lillie, why you wearing that, today?"

"Today is May 17th, Mama, my birthday."

"I know that, honey," Mama said, "but I don't think you need to go to school so dressed up. You might get paint on that sweater."

"Mama, I'm sixth grade now. I'll be careful."

"But why you have to get dressed up? That's your nicest outfit, Lillie."

There was the usual silence when Mama spoke firmly to one of them. Lillie looked around from one face to another, and only Eddie showed signs of understanding.

"Mama, on our birthdays Mr. Knox plays the violin especially for the birthday person. Everybody looks at you, and you are special. I want to be special today. Can't I, Mama?" Lillie pleaded.

"All right, Lillie," Mama answered, "but I warn you, if I come back here and find that sweater and skirt messed up you're gonna be in trouble, you hear?"

"Yes'm, Mama."

Lillie sat down, and the room became busy again. Evelyn got up to do the dishes, and Joyce went upstairs to make the beds. Now that Evelyn was in the tenth grade and Joyce in the twelfth, Mama did not have to check them any more before they went to school. Sometimes she had to remind Evelyn that she was a big girl and must not wear her skirts too short. And Mama would say that Evelyn was too young to wear all that weird makeup on her eyes.

Joyce didn't act like Evelyn. Joyce was very pretty, and Mama said she liked the way Joyce carried herself, like a nice young lady. Mama never had to remind her about too much makeup and funny-colored streaks in *her* hair. Lillie remembered the time Evelyn put some kind of medicine in her hair, and all the color came out right in front. Mama was angry, but Evelyn didn't seem to mind at all. She thought it was pretty. Lillie smiled when she thought

13

about the time Mama let Evelyn go shopping alone for shoes, and Evelyn came back with boots. Mama was going to make her take them back, but Joyce said to let Evelyn keep them—all the girls had them. Evelyn and Joyce were that way. They spoke up for each other. But Lillie felt that they treated her as though she was a baby, locking their door and whispering.

She had nobody but Mama and Michael to be really close to. Eddie was five years younger than she, and Evelyn was five years older. But she didn't really mind too much being alone. She liked Michael. He was a pretty, fat, brown baby. Mama always said he was the picture of health. He laughed all the time. Tyrone said, "Michael is what's happening."

Lillie thought of Mr. Knox. Come to think of it, maybe she had better not get to school too early after all because today was Art day, and he just might ask her to help mix the paints. They were going to blow tempera with milk straws and work with small bits of rock. Now, she would have to beg to be excused from Art to protect her clothes. She wanted to look very pretty; she also liked Art. But Mr. Knox would understand.

Yesterday, when he had placed the date on the board for today's work, she had told him the 17th of May was her birthday. He had told her May 17th was a very special day in the history of our country.

"What day?" she had asked.

"Why don't you try to find out?" That is what Mr. Knox always said. He didn't seem to know how hard it was to do

"Aw, shut up, and hurry so we can go to school," Lillie
   told Eddie.

that. But sometimes she went to the library on 103rd Street and got the librarian there to help.

Lillie had not found out about May 17th. She was more concerned about looking pretty when Mr. Knox played "Happy birthday," just for her on the violin. Sometimes two people had their birthdays on the same day. She hoped she would be the only one today. She would get to school just on time, and someone else would have to help Mr. Knox. She ate very slowly. Mama was all ready to go, and Lillie was still at the table.

"Hurry up, Lillie! Get all your things together, and don't forget your lunch. Have a happy birthday. And please don't mess up those clothes." Those were Mama's words as she walked out the door.

" 'Bye, Mama. I'll be very careful."

She finished her milk and went to get her spelling book and folder. She and Eddie walked to school together. Her sisters had already left for Jordan High.

Eddie was brushing his hair. "You think you cute," he looked at Lillie in the mirror.

"Aw, shut up, and hurry so we can go." Lillie started for the door.

"Give me my milk money," Eddie called.

"Mama didn't leave you any."

"See what you did?" Eddie slammed the front door behind them. "Mama was worrying about your old sweater and forgot to leave my money." Eddie pushed her with his shoulder.

"Stop it Eddie! You had your milk for breakfast. Shut up! And let's go."

Then one boy stood up and came over to Lillie and and started to sing, "There she is, Miss A-Mer-I-Ca." Everybody cracked up.

Mr. Knox cleared his throat rather loudly, and the room settled down. The class president got up and asked Lillie please to lead the flag salute. She was indeed special. She thought to herself that her Mama was so good to let her wear these nice clothes. Everybody loved her today. Best of all, she loved herself.

She liked leading the class in the flag salute, but whenever she was asked, she felt a little nervous. She was afraid of forgetting and saying what the big kids around Jordan Downs said: "With liberty and justice far off." She certainly wouldn't want Mr. Knox to hear her say that in class. But she wouldn't forget today; she was too happy.

On the chalk board was the date: May 17th. Mr. Knox was now before them reading that date.

"Any birthdays today?"

Lillie raised her hand and looked around. She was the only one. He went to the cupboard and took out his violin and started to play. He played the introduction, then the whole class sang.

The smile started down in her stomach and rose, slow and warm, all the way up to her lips. Lillie could feel her face burn, then her scalp tingled. How good she felt. Sort of happy, sort of shy, but oh, so good!

Then it was time to get to work. On the chalk board beside May 17th Mr. Knox had written: Supreme Court Decision Day.

Lillie was sorry now that she had not found out about

Purple paint splashed over the table and all over Lillie's sweater.

that important date. Of course, she knew that the Supreme Court was one of the three branches of the Federal Government. They studied that in the fifth grade. The Supreme Court interpreted and explained the laws. But that was all she knew. She hoped Mr. Knox would not call on her.

Nobody raised a hand when Mr. Knox asked what decision had been made by the Court on May 17th, 1954. He explained that the Court had ruled that public schools be integrated. That is, black and white children should go to school together. He told them that this created a chance for equal learning and a chance for young people to learn about each other.

While Mr. Knox talked, Lillie was thinking that she wasn't even born when that happened, so long ago. She guessed it must be a nice thing to have all kinds of people going to school together, if the Supreme Court said so. All the kids in her classroom were Negroes. She thought she should ask Mr. Knox why. But, then, almost all the people who lived in Watts were Negroes.

When it was time for the art lesson, Lillie felt she should ask to be excused. But she sat and watched the monitors spread newspapers on top of the tables and put out trays of milk cartons with mixed tempera, one on each table. Everyone was given art paper, a drinking straw, and small pieces of rocks.

Mr. Knox showed them samples: there were pictures of rocks used as fences; designs with rocks scattered throughout; and just rocks, colored with tempera, ar-

21

ranged in many forms. He told them to make anything they liked.

Lillie knew she should not work with the paint. If she got it on her clothes she would be in trouble. But she would work with only two cartons of paint, that was not much. She could do it, she thought. She would be careful, and everything would be all right.

Lillie was glad she had not asked Mr. Knox to excuse her. She decided to make a big, wide tree in black, and color her rocks pale-blue for the fence.

It was not easy to blow the tempera into the shape of a tree. The hole in the straw was small, so only a little air came out at a time. It took a long time to blow all the branches on the trunk of the tree.

The lesson was over, and her clothes were still nice and clean. The finished paintings were placed on a large strip of oil cloth on the floor to dry. It was time to clean up.

The paint monitors knew their job well. They were putting away trays and folding newspapers. One boy, carrying a paint tray, was walking by Lillie's table when another boy stood up just as he passed and hit the tray. Purple paint flew out, splashing over the table and onto Lillie's sweater.

Lillie watched the soft orange wool drink up the paint and make an ugly spot. She wanted to wipe it away frantically, but she just sat there staring. Everybody was silent.

Finally she cried out, "My mother! My mother! My sweater! I'm in trouble!" And everyone felt her anguish.

Lillie washed the sweater in warm water but the spot did not come out.

THE UGLY SPOT on her sweater became worse after Lillie got home from school. The only thing to do was to get rid of that spot. She thought of a good idea. She would wash the sweater, put it in the oven, and it would be nice and dry when Mama came home. Then Mama would never know. She had often seen Mama dry things that way. All you had to do was watch them and turn them so they would not get too hot and scorch.

Lillie washed the sweater in warm water. It felt very thick. The spot did not come out but got darker. She rubbed and rubbed. It looked better. She rinsed it in clear water under the faucet. The water got hot, and the sweater got smaller.

The oven seemed just right. She put a newspaper on the rack and placed the sweater on the paper. She turned it occasionally, but the sweater looked and felt funny. It was not soft and fluffy. It was not bright and pretty.

Joyce found her drying the sweater and told her she should never have tried to wash it. Lillie wished she didn't have to face Mama. She took the sweater and hid it under the bed. She covered her head with a blanket, and prayed Mama would not get mad at her.

The next thing she knew, Mama was shaking her. The light from the ceiling was very bright. It was dark outside. She had fallen asleep.

"Joyce said you messed up your sweater."

"I didn't mean to." Lillie sat up.

"Where is it, Lillie?"

Lillie leaned over the side of the bed and pulled out the sweater. It was wrinkled up like a dead worm. It looked toasted.

"What happened, Lillie? Child, what did you ever do to that nice sweater?" Mama was near tears.

"I'm sorry, Mama. I couldn't help it. That boy spilled the paint all over me. I tried to wash it out and messed it up like that."

"Oh, Lillie! That was the only decent thing you had!"

Lillie would have felt better if Mama had been angry. It hurt her to see Mama so sad.

Mama finally spoke, "Oh, well, did you eat your supper?"

"I don't want any. Mama, can I go?"

"Go where?"

"With you, tomorrow."

"I don't think so. You should've known better than to wash that sweater. Besides, it's beginning to rain. You stay home and think about what you did."

* * *

It was raining very hard now. Mama had just left for Mrs. Byrd's without Lillie. Big tears rolled down Lillie's

Big tears ran down Lillie's cheeks and over her chin.

cheeks and over her chin. She could feel them drop on her hand, but she refused to brush them away. She sniffed the tears back, and that was the only sound she made. She looked out the window. The other apartments were darkened by the rain. Clothes on the lines were flopping in the wind. The children's pajamas looked so funny. All the color was gone, and the plastic bottoms on the feet were hard from too much washing. They looked like puppets unwilling to dance.

Lillie went on sniffling. People hurried to and fro in the rain. Some had newspapers to shield them, others covered their heads with paper bags.

Most of the children were at home. Some, with bright yellow rain coats, were going to the store for milk and bread or sugar. But nobody came out to get a big white doll lying on the lawn. Its face was very white because it had been washed clean by the rain. The rest of its body was swollen, the mud made it dark grey. And nobody seemed to care about a quilt that had once been used for sunning.

Lillie wished she was on her way to the ocean. Her birthday, yesterday, had been one long mess. And it had started so good. She should have known better than to think it would be different.

She heard Evelyn downstairs fixing food. Joyce was home for lunch from the beauty shop where she worked on Saturdays. The day was half gone, and all Lillie had done was stand at the window and cry. She opened the bedroom door and listened.

"I brought you a copy of *Seventeen*," Joyce was saying.

"Oh, Joyce, can I keep it?" She heard Evelyn ask with a squeal of delight.

"Until I finish my lunch and go back. I borrowed it for you from the shop. Magazines are too short around there. I'll have to take it back."

Lillie thought how silly to be so excited about a magazine that showed nothing but clothes that they couldn't buy anyway. She remembered Mama telling Evelyn she had better get all those clothes out of her head. Evelyn said, without Mama hearing, that she would be happy to, when she could get some on her back. Lillie dabbed at her eyes and decided to go downstairs.

At the bottom of the stairs she could hear Eddie jumping rope inside the house. She felt like jumping too. She knew some jump rope rhymes she wanted to teach him:

> Cinderella thinks she's cute
> All she wears is a bathing suit
> If she jumps to twenty-one
> She may get another turn.

She knew another rhyme about red hot peppers:

> Cinderella dressed in yellow
> Went upstairs to kiss her fellow
> All she got was red hot peppers.

Eddie would like jumping real fast when he got to the red hot peppers. He was good at jumping rope. He liked to learn new rhymes. She would teach him. They were jumping and having a good time when Evelyn screamed at them to stop.

Eddie was good at jumping rope. Lillie
taught him some new jump rope rhymes.

"I've cleaned up this house! I don't want you in here jumping rope!"

They went right on jumping.

"Lillie, stop it, now." Evelyn was angry. "Get busy and do some work. You haven't helped at all today." Evelyn had to do the wash, and she hated washing on a rainy day.

"Don't fuss so much," Lillie said laughing. "Mama says the house is supposed to be clean enough to be healthy but dirty enough to be happy."

"Yeah, left to you, it would just be happy. Come on now and help."

"It's still Lillie's birthday celebration. Let's give her the day off," Joyce said.

"She's had all morning off. Hasn't done a thing all day." Evelyn's anger was showing.

"Leave her alone, Evelyn." The two girls went back into the kitchen and bent once more over their magazine.

* * *

It was after five o'clock before the rain really stopped. Eddie had fallen asleep downstairs, and Lillie was looking out the bedroom window again. She wished her mother would hurry home. When it rained they all worried about her because her old car was bad.

If she could have one wish, Lillie thought, it would be that she had plenty of money. The first thing she would buy would be a new car for her mother. Then Mama could go to work all over town if she wanted to and never worry about the car breaking down. Next, she would buy herself one hundred sweaters. Then she could wear one every day, and nobody would care.

30

Outside the wind had stopped blowing, and the clothes on the lines were dingy and heavy with rain. She wished there was something to do. Ordinarily, she would have Michael to play with, but Tyrone had taken him and Rosemary to visit his grandmother. They wouldn't be home until late. If it weren't raining, she and Eddie could walk up and down 103rd Street to look in the shop windows and dream.

There was no homework on weekends. She had returned the library books and hadn't taken out any more. It was hard to remember to take them back on time, and five cents a day was more than she had. So there was nothing to read.

Lillie went over to the mirror and combed her hair. She decided to make up and pretend to be a pretty lady. She closed the bedroom door and got Mama's powder and lipstick. She put on the powder. Then she put on the lipstick. She didn't do a good job. Putting on makeup always looked easy. Once she had seen a teacher put her lipstick on with a real little brush. She just painted it on. Lillie wished she had a little brush like that. She could brush lipstick on better. Everybody said she was good with paint brushes.

She brushed her hair with Mama's brush and combed and combed it. She needed an eyebrow pencil. That's what she needed. A regular pencil might do. She marked and marked. Gee, it hurt. What people go through to be pretty, she thought. She had better wash that stuff off before Mama got home.

It was getting dark. Lights were going on in the apart-

Mama brought home a big grey cat with green eyes and a great ruff like a crown.

ments. People were coming home, and Lillie could hear little children outside, happy that the rain was over.

She thought at least there was one good thing about the rain. Mr. Vital, at the nursery, would surely give her a plant now. He always said, "Wait 'til a rainy day."

There were not many rainy days in California, so he did not have to give away many plants. She would go early Monday morning and remind him. A plant would be nice in her window, she thought. And then she would have something to do, caring for the plant.

Downstairs everybody was talking at the same time. Mama was home!

Lillie ran down the stairs forgetting that she had been left home to cry all day. She was excited and glad because Mama was home.

When she entered the room, she was surprised to see a big gray cat in the middle of the table. He had green eyes and a great ruff that stood out like a crown. His tail moved slowly. Eddie was stroking the cat's fur. Eddie was happy, and the cat seemed pleased. The cat turned his eyes toward Lillie, and they stared at each other. All of a sudden the room seemed very small, and the cat seemed very large. Lillie moved to her mother and took her hand.

"He won't hurt you," Mama said. "He's a nice cat, Lillie. Why, Mrs. Byrd takes better care of that cat than some people take care of their children. Look how he takes to Eddie. He's nice, Lillie."

"But I don't like cats, Mama," Lillie said.

"Oh, you'll like this cat. He'll just spend the night. Then I'll have to take him on to the cat hospital to stay until Mrs. Byrd comes back. Imagine paying somebody to keep a cat! I should keep him here and make that money myself. No, I better not. Now, you kids listen, we can't let this cat out of this house. That cat is worth a lot of money. I'd have to work for, I don't know how long, to pay for that cat."

"Please, Mama, take him away now," Lillie begged.

"He won't bother you, Lillie, that cat is just like a baby. Sleeps in Mrs. Byrd's bed. He's a lovely cat. Look, Eddie isn't scared."

But *Lillie* was scared. She remembered when they had stayed with their grandmother before they moved to Los Angeles. Grandmother knew many stories about cats, how smart and jealous cats are; how they get too close to you and you can't breathe, and you die. She once told Lillie a story about a rich woman who owned a beautiful big grey cat with a big bushy tail. The cat had a big head, with fur standing out around it just like the cat Mama brought home. The lady would always let this cat sit at her table. Just she and the cat. The cat had everything.

Then one night this lady had company. When they sat down to eat, of course the cat came to the table, too. The lady was embarrassed. She told the cat to get down. The cat would not. The lady got mad. She hit the cat knocking him from the table.

The next day the lady was found dead in her house. Someone suggested that maybe the cat had done it. No! Not a cat! Then someone else said it could not be proved whether the cat did it or not. But no one knew for sure.

Just then, the cat Mama brought home jumped off the

The cat ran to the door and meowed and meowed.

table, and the whole house shook. Lillie trembled. That cat was just like the one her grandmother used to talk about. The eyes—same eyes. The head—just like a crown.

What could she do. She was very afraid. The cat was not tame. He was dangerous. Why was all this happening to her? she wondered. First the sweater, then the rain, no trip, and now this old cat. Surely Mama must know. She must know that cats are dangerous.

Lillie left the kitchen and went back to the bedroom. She closed the door and looked all around the room. She thought she could still feel the room shake just as it did when the cat jumped from the table. She would not go back downstairs to eat. She would go straight to bed.

Late that night, she awoke with something heavy on her feet. It was very heavy and very warm. There was a strange soft sound in the room. Purr-rr-r Purr-rr. Lillie moved toward her mother, snuggling up close. She heard a scratchy noise. Something moved up from the foot of the bed. Suddenly she felt a strange warmth up around her head. She stopped breathing. It seemed as though her heart would burst through her chest.

She tried to call her mother, but no sounds came. She tried to move and couldn't. She wanted to pull the covers over her head, but she needed air. She knew now that it was the cat. He was near her pillow. When she moved he became still. When she became still, he moved. She knew he was going to kill her.

Suddenly she leaped out of the bed. She could see nothing but his eyes shining. She could hear the strange noise. She was so afraid.

36

Now, she stood there trembling, staring that cat in the eyes. Finally, the cat leaped off the bed and the whole room shook, yet he made no sound at all. Lillie was unable to move. The cat walked to the door and said, "Meow."

She would get him out of their house. She had to. She couldn't live with the cat there. But Mama had said she mustn't let him out. Maybe she should run away, but where would she go? It was dark and wet outside. She put on her mother's robe and opened the door. She would go to sleep with Evelyn and Joyce.

When she opened the door, the cat sprang out and down the stairs. Instead of going back to bed she followed him. He went to the front door of the apartment and me-owed and me-owed.

We must never let him out, never let him out. *Never let him out.* Mama's words came to her over and over again. Yet, she went straight to the door and opened it. The cat ran through the door and was gone.

Lillie closed the door and stood with her hand over her mouth. She felt very strange. She didn't know whether she wanted to laugh or cry.

Soon she was back in bed, warm and sleepy.

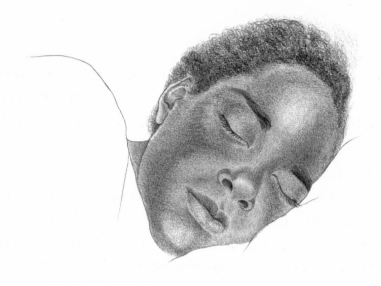

The next morning, Lillie overslept.

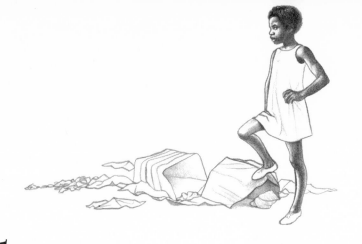

THE NEXT MORNING was Sunday. Lillie was awakened by her mother's voice. In her sleep the words seemed to push through the walls and under the crack in the door. Then she heard the words clearly.

"Lord have mercy, that cat is gone! Gone! I've been in every room in this house, and that cat isn't here. He must be here. I know he couldn't get out by himself."

Lillie heard the excited voices. First Eddie's, then all the others. Everybody was up. She had overslept.

"Go wake up Lillie," she heard her mother say. She remembered that she had let the cat out. Oh, my goodness, she thought, Mrs. Byrd will have a fit, and Mama will lose her job. Why hadn't she thought of that before. Should she tell? Mama would surely beat her if she knew what she had done. She would play asleep, she thought. She pulled the covers up and closed her eyes as Eddie bounded up the stairs.

"Lillie!" She didn't move. "Lillie, Mama says get up!" Eddie shook her.

Still she didn't move.

"Mama," he yelled, "she won't get up!"

"Tell her she had better!"

"You heard her, Lillie," Eddie said. "You'd better get up. Mama is mad. The cat is gone."

"Leave me alone. I don't care if that old cat is gone."

"You better get out of that bed." And Eddie ran back down the stairs.

Lillie rolled over and put her feet solidly on the floor. She dressed, but instead of going downstairs, she sat down on the edge of the bed. She could hear muffled voices downstairs.

"Lillie, you come on down here!" Mama shouted.

She got up and walked slowly down the stairs into the kitchen.

"Morning," she said without smiling.

"Lillie, I can't find that cat," Mama greeted her.

"Where'd you look, Mama?" Lillie's voice surprised herself. She went on quickly, "Maybe he's hiding somewhere. Did you look under everything?" She stood in the center of the room with her hands on her hips. That is what Mama always did when she wanted to appear important.

"I've looked all over. Under everything. He's not in this house," Mama answered.

Lillie moved to the cupboard to get a plate. Everyone else had eaten breakfast. The plates were still on the table with bits of bacon rinds and grits and smudges of jam on them.

The food was still warm, but the grits had settled firmly in the pot. Lillie liked creamy grits, hot enough to melt the butter. Now she wished she had been the first

"Lillie, I can't find that cat," Mama said. She seemed very
worried and upset.

one in the pot. She spooned the eggs out on the plate and picked up the last strip of bacon. They always had a good breakfast on Sunday morning.

Everyone was quiet. Lillie was about to take the last bite when Mama said, "Lillie, did you let that cat out?"

"No'm, Mama." She kept her eyes on her plate.

"I heard you up last night. What were you doing?

"You heard me . . . ?"

"Yes, I heard you, and the cat was in the room. But I was so sleepy. What did you do? I sorta remember your getting up. You let that cat out, didn't you, Lillie?"

"Yes'm, Mama." She looked at Mama with sad eyes.

"Why would you do a thing like that, girl?" Mama exploded.

"I don't know."

"You don't know?" Mama cried. "Oh, Lillie! Don't I have enough trouble? I have to take that cat back, and you let him out. If my old car hadn't broken down, I would have gotten there before the cat hospital closed for the night. That's an expensive cat, Lillie. I'll never be able to get another one like it. Now you hurry up and get out of here and find that cat, you hear me? And don't come back without him!"

Lillie went down 103rd Street. As she passed the nursery she noticed that the fence was broken near the ground. She crawled under. Maybe the cat was in there, hiding in the shade house.

She was very nervous and afraid when she got inside. The nursery was forbidden territory. The only time they

42

Lillie stepped carefully among the bottles that had been thrown over the nursery fence Saturday night.

were allowed within those gates was when their class was invited with their teacher.

Nobody was around. She moved cautiously, stepping carefully among the bottles that had been thrown over the fence Saturday night. The place seemed deserted.

The door into the house with the glass top was not locked. She went in. It was nice and warm in there. That was where they grew the plants from seeds and cuttings. But the cat wasn't there. She closed the door behind her and went on to the shade house. The floor was covered with potted plants. "Kitty," she called, "here, kitty." There was no answer.

Lillie looked outside among the gallon cans. She looked along the fence near the bird of paradise plants, and among the bottle brushes. She had never seen a bottle brush before. It had a long stem with red things sticking out like the hairs on Mama's brush. "Here kitty," she called again.

Lillie looked in the natal plum bushes. One summer Mr. Vital had given her and Eddie a plum from that bush. A red, soft fruit. Real soft inside with tiny seeds. There was no fruit on the bushes now. There were only white flowers with a very sweet smell.

She went back to the fence, but the cat was not there. She wished she could pick up all those bottles. She and Eddie could take them to the store and get some money for them. But right now she had to find that cat. She squeezed back out onto the sidewalk.

Her dress was muddy now, but she went on. She crossed to the other side of the street. The Tobacco Road

*Lillie was afraid to ask the policeman
if he'd seen the large, grey cat.*

Shoe Shop was closed up tight. She looked behind Harvey's Live Poultry Shop thinking the cat might be there. Nothing but a few feathers. At the Tops Loan Company iron gates covered the windows. Lillie peeped through the bars to see what was in the window. The guitar she and Eddie had wanted was gone.

When she passed the police station, a policeman was standing in the door. She almost asked him if he had seen a large, grey cat. But she thought better of it. Suppose he thought she was playing a game or had lost her mind? Where would she get a cat that looked like that? She hurried past him, glad she hadn't found it yet, so she wouldn't have to explain to him what she was doing with an expensive cat like that in Watts.

Farther on Lillie came to a park. There was a big sign with the words on it: WILL ROGERS MEMORIAL PARK, COUNTY OF LOS ANGELES. She crossed the grass and looked around the big rocks and through the plants and flowers. She called, "Kitty, kitty, where are you, kitty?" Near the walk was a big concrete square. It was supposed to be for concerts, but Lillie had never heard anyone play there. She had read in a book that bands play beautiful music in parks and people read stories. But if they did that at Will Rogers' she had never heard about it. She stood in the middle of the big stone square and said as loudly as she could, "Where are you, old cat?"

Avoiding puddles of water on the cement, she walked over to the swings. The leather seats were dark with water stains, but Lillie didn't mind. Up and down she

She was having so much fun on the swings she forgot all about looking for the cat.

pumped herself forgetting why she had come to the park. The air smelled fresh and clean after the rain. The sky was clear and blue. The sun was bright, and mocking-birds were singing.

Lillie sang too. "Baby, everything's all right." She was sailing high when she remembered the cat. Shoving her foot down to stop the swing, ouch! she hurt her ankle. She jumped off the swing and started out of the park. She discovered she had really hurt her ankle.

Lillie crossed to the other side of 102nd Street and kept walking. There were just houses here. She walked slowly, looking carefully for the cat. There were two cats on a porch. Maybe her cat was there too. She opened the wire gate slowly, for she was afraid of the cats. One was stretched out sleeping on the wooden porch in front of the door. The other was on the railing licking his paws and washing his face. She walked cautiously up the steps. The sleeping cat, frightened by Lillie, woke up and ran away. The other one just sat and stared at her.

The house was very quiet. She knocked softly at first. Then she banged on the door, but nobody came. It was too early on Sunday morning, Lillie thought. She walked out the gate and on down the street.

Mama was sure mean, she thought. Why did she, Lillie, have to be out so early looking for a cat? Mama never should have brought it home. What if something happened to her, Lillie thought. Then Mama would be sorry she had made her go out to look for that old cat.

She crossed a vacant lot with bricks and burned-out rubble left from the time when they had all that trouble in Watts. Lillie remembered the nights when the fires were burning, and policemen were shooting and sirens screaming. Then the soldiers had come. It was just like the war pictures she had seen on television.

But the cat wasn't here. She picked up a brick and let it fall on a bottle shattering it. She walked on.

An old man was sitting on a porch with his hands folded in his lap, his eyes closed.

"Morning," Lillie said to him. "Did you see a big gray cat come by here?"

"No, I didn't; not this morning. Where you live?" He sat up and placed his hands under his knees.

"Jordan Downs Housing Project," Lillie answered.

"Away off there? Must be some cat to bring you all the way down here so early."

"It is, and it doesn't belong to us. B'longs to the lady my Mama works for," Lillie answered.

"Oh, that kinda cat. Well, don't think you'll find him here. He won't stay any longer in Watts than he has to." The man laughed.

Lillie began to think he was right. But I've got to find him, she thought.

Now the streets were coming alive. People were out, going to church. They were all dressed up. This time last Sunday she had been dressed in her nice skirt and sweater. But she didn't want to think about that sweater. She walked on to the railroad tracks.

When she got to the railroad tracks, she tried to walk on the rails, but it was difficult because her ankle hurt. She soon gave up; besides there was a lot of gravel to hurt

It was early Sunday morning and the streets of Watts were deserted. Mama was sure mean, she thought. Why did she have to be out so early looking for a cat?

Lillie had been warned to stay away from the junk yards around Alameda Street.

her hands and knees if she fell, and there was broken glass too. She left the rails and headed back towards Jordan High School.

Where could that cat be? She didn't know where to look anymore. Her ankle was hurting, but she had to go on. "Don't come back 'til you find that cat. Don't come back, find that cat," burned in her mind.

Lillie went past the school toward the junk yards around Alameda Street. She had been warned to stay away from them. They were very dangerous.

"That stuff's piled up so high," her mother said once, "if you breathe hard on it it'll come tumbling down and crush you."

There was a mountain of tin strips there. She and Eddie often argued about who could climb it the fastest. A cat might like to get in there and hide.

A car had knocked the fence loose during an accident. Lillie walked into the junk yard. The big crane that tossed old cars on top of a heap was still, now. Its long neck was stiff, and the gaping jaws were closed. Lillie walked around it with great respect. She was about to look for the cat in an old car when a voice called: "Hey, come outa there! Right now, come out! You'll get hurt!" There was Mr. Vital.

Lillie started out. He met her near the opening in the fence.

"What are you doing in there?" Mr. Vital asked.

"I'm looking for a cat." Lillie felt very tired now and her ankle hurt. "It isn't my cat, but it's my fault he ran away. I *have* to find him."

"Well it's plain you don't know nothing about cats," said Mr. Vital. "Cats won't go in places like that. Whose cat is it?" His sharp black eyes were smiling in spite of his words.

"Belongs to the lady my Mama works for." Lillie's tears were near the surface.

"Well, let me tell you something about cats," said Mr. Vital. "They won't go far from the place where they get loving care. Did you take good care of him?" He smiled down in sympathy at Lillie.

"No, sir. I was scared of him. Cats get too close and you can't breathe and you die; my grandmother told me so," Lillie said without taking a breath.

"Why Lillie," Mr. Vital seemed surprised. "How could that be? I've had cats all my life and they never did anything like that. Did your grandma ever have a cat for a pet?"

"No," Lillie said, "I'm sure she never did."

"Well, then, you see," Mr. Vital answered, "she couldn't know for sure whether that's true or not. But I can tell you it's not true. Cats make good pets, if you love them and take good care of them."

"If people like 'em then they like people?" asked Lillie.

"Sure," Mr. Vital laughed. "Your being scared of the cat made the cat scared of you, poor cat."

"Poor me," said Lillie. "I can't go home 'til I find that cat."

Mr. Vital thought for a moment. "Cats are easily scared," he said. "Maybe he started to run away, got

"It's plain you don't know nothing about cats," Mr. Vital told Lillie.

frightened and ran under your house. Have you looked there yet?"

"No, but I looked just about every place else," answered Lillie.

"Go look around your house," Mr. Vital said. "And Lillie, if you find him, don't be afraid of him because, wherever he is, he's pretty scared himself. I'm sure he's hoping that you'll come and pick him up and love him and take him back inside."

"Do you really think so?" Lillie asked. "Do you think he's more scared than me?"

"Of course," Mr. Vital answered. "Cats are nice. Nice clean animals. Cleanest pets you can have. I tell you what, run on home. Your cat just might be 'round there."

Mr. Vital headed north on Alameda Street, and Lillie headed south. When she turned the corner on 103rd Street she realized she couldn't go home. Suppose the cat wasn't there. She couldn't face her Mama without him.

Jordan High School steps seemed a nice place to sit. She was very tired, and her ankle hurt. She sat on the steps. The tears came, and she couldn't stop them. Lillie folded her arms on her knees, placed her head on her arms and cried. She cried and cried. "Kitty please come back. Please come back. I'll be nice. I'll love you. Mama, I'm sorry."

She didn't know how long she sat there. Suddenly she heard her Mama saying softly, "Lillie, Lillie, what's the matter? I was worried about you. Where have you been?"

"Oh, Mama!" and the tears started all over again. "I

can't find that cat, Mama. I've looked everywhere. Is it at home, Mama?"

"No, he's not."

"But what if I don't find him, Mama?"

"Well, then you don't find him."

"But Mama, Mrs. Byrd will be mad at you."

"Yes, she may be mad at me."

"And you'll lose your job, Mama."

"Mrs. Byrd loves that cat very much. That cat to her, I think, is sorta like you and Eddie to me. I hope we'll find it for her."

"But Mama, if we don't. . . ."

"That won't be the worst thing that could happen to us, Lillie. I would like for you to find the cat, then you would feel better because you know you did wrong. But if you don't, we'll just have to face whatever happens."

"Mama, I'm sorry. But I was so scared of that cat. It jumped on me last night and I was afraid it would get too close and I couldn't breathe. That's what Grandma told me cats did. But Mr. Vital says that isn't true. What do you think, Mama?"

"Poor Lillie." Mama hugged her. "So that's why you let the cat out. That's an old story people used to tell about cats, but it's not true. I don't think Grandma believed it herself. I guess she didn't think you would either."

"Oh," Lillie smiled. "I'm glad it's not true. But, Mama, what are we going to do now?"

"Well," Mama answered, "don't worry. Remember, if we don't find him, he's only a cat. People are more impor-

As Mama and Lillie neared home, Eddie ran around the brick wall of the project. In his arms was the magnificent cat.

tant than cats. I can get another job if I have to. But I could never find another little girl like you."

Lillie snuggled against her mother. She thought of all the things that had happened to her since her birthday. She looked at Mama, and a deep smile started way down inside of her. And she thought again—people are more important than cats, sweaters, and cars. If she could make one wish now, she would wish that all the children in Jordan Downs and all over Watts and the world had a mama like hers.

"Mama, Mr. Vital says cats hide near where they are loved. He said that cat might be right up under the house."

"Let's look," said Mama.

Mama took both of Lillie's hands and helped her down the high steps of the school. Lillie walked slowly, leaning heavily on her mother's arm.

As they neared home, Eddie ran around the brick wall of the project. In his arms was the magnificent cat.

"Mama! Lillie! I found him! I found him near the house! Here he is!"

The cat jumped from Eddie's arms and ran toward Mama and Lillie. Not thinking, Lillie reached for the cat.

"Don't let him get away," she said excitedly as she held the cat awkwardly.

"He won't go away." Mama reached over and took the cat in her arms. "He's happy to see us. He's been alone for a long time."

He was nice and soft. Lillie seemed surprised.

"He's happy, too. Listen to him." Mama stroked him gently.

Lillie smiled as she realized the cat would not hurt her. The big, grey cat purred.

"What's that sound, Mama?" Lillie asked.

"He's purring, silly," Eddie answered quickly.

"Yes, he's happy to be back," Mama smiled.

Lillie reached out a timid hand and stroked the long silken fur. "Oh, Mama, I'm glad he's back, too."

"Here, give him to me." Eddie reached for the cat with wide open arms. "Sure wish he was mine."

"Let me hand him to Eddie, Mama," Lillie said shyly. She gently took the cat and passed him into Eddie's waiting arms. The cat put its paws on Eddie's shoulder and rubbed its head against his ear. Lillie reached out her hand and stroked its head. The cat purred contentedly and Lillie smiled. "Oh, Mama, I think I'm beginning to love him, too," she said.